THE HUNTSMAN AT THE GATE

THE HUNTSMAN
AT THE GATE

ALMET JENKS

ILLUSTRATED BY
EDWARD SHENTON

WITH A FOREWORD BY
RONALD TREE

LONDON
VICTOR GOLLANCZ
1953

Printed in Great Britain by
The Camelot Press Ltd., London and Southampton

FOREWORD

by

RONALD TREE

I HAVE NEVER MET a hunting man who at some time or another has not asked himself the question "What must it be like to be hunted? To have twenty-five couples of hounds gradually getting nearer, and at the same time knowing that there is some heavy plough ahead before sanctuary can be reached and the added knowledge, which I am sure foxes possess to a high degree, that scent on this particular day is breast high?" I well remember, though it is well over twenty years ago, a memorable hunt while I was Joint-Master of the Pytchley—fifty minutes as hard as you could go over one of the finest bits of country in England— late on a February evening. We lost our fox as darkness came, but a few days later he was dis- covered dead in the covert in which we had found him, his lungs filled with pneumonia. Yet, I think, it would be a mistake to suppose that foxes always suffer from being the hunted ones. Experience has taught me to believe that when scent is poor, which it very often is, and when the initiative lies with them, they positively enjoy the contest in which they almost invariably come out best.

There is something of the whimsical combined with an eeriness bordering on the supernatural in foxes. It is the combination of these traits that Mr. Almet Jenks has described so delightfully in this volume for which I have been asked to write a brief foreword.

For those in Britain who have never had the opportunity to hunt the fox in the United States, a word of explanation is necessary. The grey fox which Mr. Jenks describes is an animal utterly unlike his red counterpart. Although he derives from the same common family, he has never been known to cross with a red fox. His characteristics are different. When hunted, he seldom, if ever, goes straight and generally runs in small circles amongst the underbrush, and when in danger takes to the branches of a high tree like a cat. Many years ago, when I was very young, I kept a pack of hounds in the mountains of Virginia where only grey foxes live. The hounds were a scratch lot used to hunting by themselves and ill adapted to discipline of any kind. Some English friends, fresh from the wide expanses of Leicestershire, came to stay and I was naturally anxious to show sport. Unfortunately, on the way to the meet, the hounds picked up a cold trail, i.e. where a grey fox had crossed several hours before. They were off at once and we never did reach our meeting place. But worse was in store, for after a fast hunt through some dense underbrush an animal was eventually treed the hounds excitedly baying as American hounds do only to discover to my intense mortification that they had been hunting a large, grey tom cat.

THE HUNTSMAN AT THE GATE

"GO SINK THE WIND!" said the huntsman, who had been reading some old books on fox hunting. He spoke to his second whipper-in and—for his own enjoyment—in a tone of voice one might use in saying, "Go and climb a tree!" He went on quickly, "Try and get a view. Be ready to stop 'em if it's—if it's a racing leopard or something. It's like no fox *I* ever knew."

That had been three hours ago, at a short check. The field—the few that were left—were in earshot at the time, and it amused the huntsman a little to think that none of them, probably, would have any idea what the order to the whip meant. Nor would the whip, at first—the expression was long out of date—but would understand at the second command: "Try and get a view." As expected, the whip looked blank, then nodded quickly, but did not make off. In this particular hunt, the huntsman ran the show; as little discretion as possible was committed to the staff, in the field, in the kennels and stables. So the whip waited for further directions.

"Gallows Corner," the huntsman said without hesitation. This might be quite wrong, of course, but it seemed the best bet—considering the way the quarry had been running. A decision had to be made at once, and he was the one to make it. He said, "That'll give you a view of the road for half a mile."

The whip touched his hunting crop to the peak of his velvet cap, turned his horse, trotted a few steps, put the horse into a gallop and made straight for the highway. The few followers left in the field watched him go thudding by, the hound couples dancing up and down against his horse's flank. What this manœuvre meant they had no idea, but they were careful to show no sign of ignorance. They kept quiet and looked wise and stayed carefully away from hounds at all times—a well-disciplined field, knowing little of the art, the science, of the sport but

12

wonderfully conversant with its proper dress and peculiar language.

The whip's way was straight down wind, well out on the flank of the nearly straight line that the fox—or whatever the hunted animal might be—was taking, and fast, but at the same time saving his horse as much as possible, along the grassy shoulder of the highway, which fortunately ran that way, to the high crest on the turnpike, known as Gallows Corner. Here, far down wind and far ahead of the hunting hounds, and in great loneliness—for this was a strange and sparsely settled part of the country—he would sit his horse and keep his eyes glued to the half-mile of track that crossed a roughly straight prolongation of the line that hounds were now hunting. Posted there, sometimes standing in his stirrup-irons, leaning forward—he would stare so hard he would be seeing things, all kinds of wild creatures—he would, if the huntsman had guessed right, first hear in the distance the faint, wonderful music of the pack. Nearer and nearer, swelling, rising to a great crashing chorus, it would come, and the whipper-in, half-blind now from

13

gazing, would suddenly see—and his heart would be in his throat—the tired red fox slowly, deliberately pick his way across the road . . . or, if not a fox, then a racing leopard or water-buffalo or some strange beast that had escaped from the circus when it left town last summer.

But the second whip got a view of nothing that day. He heard hounds once, far, far off, and then not again. He saw no one, no living creature. Darkness came soon in these short winter days, and night followed fast—no moon that night, no stars—and he could not have seen an elephant cross the road. He stayed till dark, and now the hunt must be far away or blown off, and there was nothing more he could do out there, so he walked his horse down to the highway and began the ten-mile-or-so ride home.

After the whip had galloped off, the huntsman sat motionless on his big bay horse, never touching his horn, watching hounds make their cast. There was no question, no doubt in his mind: one of the old, trusted hounds—Artful, say, or Mermaid or

14

Mournful—would pick up the line in a moment—
no check that day had lasted more than a minute
or two—and they would be off again—to where,
God alone knew! They had been running from a
quarter past two that afternoon, and it was now
going on to four, but it was not so much the elapsed
time as the terrible pace the quarry had imposed.
The sun would set shortly after four and they could
go on for a little while after that, and then they
would be benighted. Yet the huntsman could not
bear to whip hounds off the line or blow them off
during one of the infrequent checks. They had had
little luck so far, that season, and their season of

hunting was, at best, a short one. The young entry —four and a half couple of them were out that day —needed blooding. At the same time, he knew that, mounted—he was thinking now of himself and the whipper-in that remained to him, not of the field —they could not follow hounds across country, over fence and ditch and brook, in the dark. But if this were a grey fox they were hunting, a quarry that usually ran in circles, he and the first whip could turn their horses over to someone in the field who would take their horses home, and then huntsman and whip could go on, on foot, all night if necessary. *If* it had been a grey fox.

But of course it wasn't, but was certainly the red fox of the world—or maybe a racing leopard, springbok, hartebeest. . . . Deer, the huntsman didn't like even to think of. There were deer in the country, all right. Where were they not?—the gentle, soft-eyed . . . he had several names for them, none printable. They had deer—tame ones—in the kennel run, to break hounds to them, and hounds paid little attention to these four-footed friends in kennels, and the huntsman knew he could have lifted his pack intact through a deer-park, but let hounds be running a fox, with their blood really up, and let a deer cross that line, and—goodbye, boys! The scent of deer was, apparently, far more ravishing; deer, after all, was their more natural quarry.

But, despite the day's burning pace and the straight line and this strange country they were coming to, where foxes did not usually dwell, the huntsman was almost sure it was not deer. He could have given you several reasons for this belief: the way the old, trusted hounds were hunting, the voices of certain hounds and the cry of the pack, the way they cast and, once the line was owned, the way they ran. It was his business to know all these things, and these things were, now, his whole life. But, like a truly great commander, he tried to button everything up. This was a grass country and the few roads they had crossed were iron hard and took no impression of pad or hoof or foot, so neither he nor his two whips—no one in the field, he suspected (any possible Boy Scouts being in school), knew enough to tell the print of a rabbit from a skunk—had been able to prick the hunted animal. Therefore, in the

hope of making absolutely sure, the huntsman had
sent his second whip far down wind to an observa-
tion post on a road that the huntsman had good
reason to think the quarry would cross. If it turned
out *not* to be a fox, then the whipper-in would
instantly gallop to the point on the road where the
hunted animal, whatever it was, had crossed, and
there take his stand, whip ready, and when the

leading hounds appeared would, if he could not get ahead and stop them, ride in among them, very much as would a mounted policeman among a crowd of rioters, smack his whip and rate them in shrill, angry screams and so try to stop them and hold them there while the huntsman and the other whip came on to him.

As the huntsman watched the cast, a member of the field, sometimes referred to, when not present, as the Rubber Baron or "that shad-bellied" (meaning, not his conformation, but the style of his scarlet field-coat) "so-and-so," walked his almost beaten horse over to him. The huntsman, who was never mysterious or oracular about his tactical moves, explained briefly the mission of the second whip.

"Oh, a fox, I'm sure," the Baron said confidently. "And a straight-necked one, what?" This was straight out of Surtees, the expensive, scarlet-and-gold edition; the Baron, an Anglomaniac, had not quite dared "straight-necked 'un." The huntsman, keeping his eye on hounds, said, "I'd take that horse in, if I were you, sir." There was no trace of servility in the huntsman's use of "sir." He was, in a sense, in the other's employ, for the Baron was a very large subscriber of the hunt and the "keeping up" of the country. And the huntsman—he was only human, after all—preferred to maintain the barrier between them, happy, in this case, to be on a separate, if lower level. For the huntsman was a gentleman—if the term be allowed—that had come down in the world, while the Baron was another kind of man that had come up.

"Oh, he's just blown a bit," the Baron said now, referring to the condition of his horse.

"He's lame, sir," said the huntsman shortly.

As he spoke, Mournful spoke too, in her high, thin voice, and then Dawdle and Gamin, and the rest closed on these three, and now the fourth and last movement of the symphony swelled to one tremendous chorus. The huntsman shortened his reins and closed his legs on the tired horse. He stuck the gleaming copper horn between the breast-buttons of his scarlet coat and rode for what looked like a gap at the end of a low, broken-down stone wall. He thanked God in his heart that they were in a far, outlying country where the hunt did not keep up the fences and build up the stone walls. To stay with hounds and still save the aged hunter he rode. . . . A worn grass wagon-track led into the next field, across which hounds were streaming in full cry. The huntsman, hating it, closed his legs sharply, just touching his blind spurs to the lathered flanks. The old horse broke into a gallop. The rider, getting himself out of the saddle, leaned far forward to free the tired quarters. Behind him came the four that were left of the field. The Baron was no longer among them, the master was not there—he had had a fall earlier in the run, nothing serious, but the delay, in view of the pace, was fatal—but— the huntsman did not have to look back to see—the master's daughter would, somehow, follow to the end.

All that day, and especially during the last few hours, the huntsman wished he could lose the field. Then, good and lost, they would go safely home. He had wished this—as he wished it now—because of the master's daughter. She was not good with a horse—she was a beginner, really—and here she

was today, upon a flashy-looking chestnut that went boiling into his fences . . . the huntsman had a way of seeing these things—when it came to her, anyway. The girl rode side-saddle, and the chestnut, obviously, didn't like it, didn't like the strange skirt, streamlined though it was, and resented the uneven weight, for she did not ride well. What could the huntsman do? He scarcely knew her—it was his first season with this pack—but once he had spoken to her about a beautiful, worthless brown horse that some coper had unloaded on her father to the tune of three or four thousand dollars, probably. One morning in the early cubbing season she had been having a hellish time with the horse, and when the huntsman told her she should get rid of the animal, the tears of defeat came into her eyes, and he was sorry then that he had spoken. The huntsman liked the girl—what he saw of her—and he wondered at her courage in keeping on with something that she did not really care for and that she probably feared. For he suspected—although she put on a good show of being calm and cool—that most of the time out hunting she was afraid. You might think that this would have lowered her in his eyes, but the huntsman had reason to know that one could face a withering enemy fire coolly enough and yet shudder at the thought of a steep rock climb.

Perhaps she had, inadvertently, betrayed this fear to him. The facts of the case were simple, but the resulting situation was terribly complicated. The master's daughter, his only child, heiress to one of the great fortunes—her mother had died when the girl was very young—had fallen in love with the huntsman. He would never have imagined such a thing, had it not been for a young man, a member of the hunt, who, coming to the kennels one night about a hunt matter—walking hound puppies, or something—and having had plenty to drink, had told the huntsman what a good part of the country-side were talking about. The huntsman was dread-fully embarrassed and troubled to hear this. He was a poor man—he had nothing put away, really nothing; his sole means of living was the salary paid him as a professional huntsman. . . .

All his friends would tell you that he had simply had bad luck: the small business he had put his small capital into had failed, and the hunt he then hunted with, having suddenly lost its professional huntsman, offered him the job, to tide things over. Hunting hounds was an art and a science that he took to, so he stayed on the job another year, and another year after that. Then *that* hunt folded up when a few rich people abruptly withdrew their support for reasons having to do with the social hierarchy—reasons that the huntsman never did fathom—and he counted himself lucky indeed, though he was duly sorry, when the huntsman of a neighbouring pack had a fall—not over a fence, not even in the field, but at a walk on a hard greasy road —had both legs crushed, no chance of ever riding again, was pensioned off, and the job offered *him*.

And now the waters were all muddied again, by a foolish, pretty girl. Yes, he would have to admit her prettiness . . . her beauty—to him, anyway—when dressed up in the dark blue side-saddle habit, little hard hat, veil, and the rest—a costume that would not appeal to everyone, in a rôle for which she was totally unfitted.

What could the huntsman do about it? He could, their small world said, run off with the girl and marry her; she would ride at a five-foot stone wall (with her eyes shut) if he told her to. So it was generally believed that a wedding over the border would be the upshot—the huntsman could count on being taken care of in some way. But, to be fair to him, this never entered his mind. He liked the girl and he was angry to see her torturing herself over a mere sport. Even if he had fallen in love with her—and he would have thought that foolish to suppose, she being for one thing so much younger than he, about twenty, a mere child, really—even in that case, a marriage, with the heiress aspect and all the complications, was out of the question. It would be too embarrassing.

Two fields further on, hounds turned right-handed in a wide arc, taking the curve at top speed. The huntsman pulled up, expecting them to swing down wind again, but they kept straight on, and with louder cry, across the light wind, which was blowing from the north. As the afternoon waned and the air grew colder than the sun-warmed earth, scent had improved—that was one theory, and it seemed to be working out today. Now the sun was already behind the foothills to the southwest, and scent was burning. Suddenly they burst into a strange country—strange to the huntsman, anyway. But he could not be expected to know all that vast country in his first season, and, as he galloped, he glanced back at the field with the idea, the first chance he got, to ask where they were: what about this country? any precipices? any bottomless chasms? Any—and he saw that there was no one left but that damned girl—no, he didn't mean that. She was all right; a trouble, a worry, that was all. His first whip was out on the left flank somewhere. The whip—and the huntsman didn't think much of his judgment—might know this country and know what he was doing: the best place for him to ride with only one whip remaining. As for the second whip and his lonely vigil at Gallows Corner, he was lost for good this day, and no great loss, either.

The huntsman decided he would not question the girl as to where they were. In any case, there was no stopping hounds at this point. He would not stop them—if he could—even though the quarry was heading straight for the fiery furnace. For any instant now—so you would have thought—they might break from scent to view, and the day would be saved. There was every chance. If they could bowl him over here in this open country before he reached. . . . What was that, ahead? In the quickening dusk it looked like the great wall of China.

That was the trouble, the dark. If they could beat the darkness, if they could kill before night. . . . The huntsman felt his heart lift. This might be his lucky day. In a way, he had it coming; so far, this year, he had had so little luck.

And then—such was their fierce, burning pace— Gamin and Warrior, the leading hounds now—he could still recognize them in the fast-fading light— were closing the wall; the rest of the pack on their very heels. The wall, the huntsman saw as he came

on, was a high board fence, boards so close together
as to show little or no daylight between and to
appear, in the dusk and at a distance, a solid grey
wall. He saw Gamin leap at the fence and be
instantly thrown back, as if by some unseen barrier.
Warrior, Sambo, Mournful followed, and two of
them went over, sprawling, and the huntsman saw
then the strand of wire stretched from post to post,
a foot above the top board. Hounds were charging
the fence, scrambling up, falling backwards, leaping

29

again with fierce, angry cry. Most of them managed to get under the wire—some actually clawed their way over it.

The huntsman rode up—it was new barbed wire, he saw now—and he was about to dismount to cut the wire when he realized that by the time he had done so, hounds would all be over, even the new entry, who were having the worst of it. But he would have to cut the wire, anyway, to jump the fence, and he freed his right foot from the iron——

Suddenly he thought of the lone girl behind him; she was just waiting to follow him over, on that fool horse. How had she lasted this long? Even without the wire, the fence was terribly high. He judged it was a shade under five feet, and he was a good judge; men that hunted and rode races over timber had a marvellous eye for picking that part of a fence a fraction of an inch lower. . . . Almost all the hounds were over the fence now. . . . It was not the kind of fence you met with in a fair hunting country, in spite of the loose talk that goes around about five-foot fences.

He looked right and left; the wire ran in both

directions—and then he saw, some distance off to the left, but not clear in the half-light, what he had not noticed at first: a break of some kind in the uniform height of the fence. He turned and galloped down the fence line.

It was a gate, not quite so high as the fence, and chained and padlocked. For some reason—he did not stay to wonder why—extending upwards a few feet from each gatepost was a dead tree-limb that looked as if it had been nailed to the post. It was a five-barred gate, showing plenty of daylight—what little was left. A nasty thing to get tangled up in. He turned the big bay horse and rode him back a little from the gate to place him for the jump. He thought of the girl again, who had followed him down the fence line. Hounds had gone on, on the other side. Cry was fading, fading. He must get on, too. He owed her nothing. It was her choice. It was her own——

"Will you help me, please?" he said, turning to her and speaking fast. "The fox is sure to turn left-handed—down wind again. Ride down this fence" —he pointed with his whip—"to the corner." If

31

there is a corner, he thought; there must be a corner. "Then turn right and ride along the fence—*stay outside the fence*. If you try to get inside, you may head him. See if you can get a view."

"What are you going to do?" she asked him. Behind the veil, her eyes looked enormous in the dusk.

"I'll be with hounds."

"Please, I'd like to stay with hounds," she said, staring at him. "You have a whip out there on the left."

"I don't know where *he* is," the huntsman said, raging. She was not so dumb, for a pretty girl all dressed up in dark blue, white stock—— He was trying to keep her from getting hurt. Time was running out.

"*Will* you go?" he said in cold anger. He put everything he had into these words. "If it's the last thing I ask you, will you go *now*?"

She gave him one look, turned her horse, touched him on the flank with her coiled whip and rode off into the darkness. Not quite straight and easy in the saddle, she would never be really good. Well, there were other fields, other diversions, such as love, marriage. . . .

The huntsman gathered his tired horse to put him at the gate, and suddenly, for no reason that he could name, in that moment of time, everything seemed to go to pieces inside him. There is the old tale of the drowning man who sees his whole life unwind before him in the little while he takes to drown, and it was like this now with the huntsman. The thoughts crowded in: It would be dark in ten minutes and he would have to whip hounds off—if he could—alone, probably—the best line they'd had all year. He should have done it earlier, when it was still light; a bad mistake. All his life he had made mistakes, one after another, and he had got no-where. What was he, who was to have done such wonderful, fine things? A huntsman of hounds! Paid servant of a . . . what did they say about it? "Cruel, artificial, rich man's sport"—how often he had defended it against these charges! . . . And that girl's face when she had looked at him a moment ago—he was not a complete damned fool, and he could see her whole soul staring out of her eyes, and he knew the trouble she would make for him. A great, vast, terrible despair closed down——

"Over we go, old man," he said to the tired horse and rode at the gate. He thought she was a pretty girl, and if things had been different, he rich, and she poor——

He felt the big bay hunter put in one tremendous thrust and then—too late—the huntsman saw the wire—a strand of wire between the two tree-limbs that ran upwards from the gateposts. He ducked, but the wire caught him anyway, across the eyes, and jerked him back. He let the reins go, but not quick enough, for the old horse hit hard—a terrible, splintering crash, an instant of blinding, searing pain, and the sudden dark.

HE WAS ALONE, on foot, in the dark. At first he thought it was his eyes—that he had been blinded, and he pulled off his right glove and put his right hand gingerly up to his eyes, to see if he could tell, by feel, how bad the wound was. He felt his eyes and face, and his eyes seemed to be all right —he could see his hand, now that his eyes were getting used to the dark—and there was no wetness from blood nor any wound at all, so far as he could tell. He thought that strange, for he had taken the wire right across his eyes—and then he thought that this was a dream, that he was not, could not be, really whole and unhurt, and that in a moment he would wake to the reality of blindness and pain; he must face the consequences of that terrible fall. Or was the fall—was all that, the gate and the wire and, before that, that tremendous run, and all the rest, but a dream? He shook his head, to clear it, to get things straight. And who but a fiend would string a single strand of wire between those two sticks running up from the gateposts? What could be the purpose? In broad daylight anyone could see the wire. Only because of the failing light had he failed to see it. Had the wire been strung there for just this one contingency—that someone would try to jump the gate in the semi-darkness? As he had tried.

He stood there, listening, straining his ears. He could have heard one of his hounds speak if it was half a world away. Now he heard not the faintest sound of hounds hunting. He had lost them completely.

The huntsman could see better in the dark now, and he saw that he must have wandered away from the broken gate and the board fence for there was no sign of either. Nor was there sign or sound of his horse. The old fool had probably gone trotting off, reins dangling, the way horses do in their dumb way after a fall, after you've pulled their legs out from under a fence rail, off they go, not waiting for *you*, without so much as a thank you. His hunting whip had gone. This was a stag-handled, silver-ringed affair, a gift from the other hunt, and he thought of trying to look for it, but then he knew it would be hopeless, in the dark. The copper horn still stuck fast between the breast-buttons of his coat.

What to do? Which way to go in a strange country? He looked up, but no stars were out. The wind, which had been blowing from the north, had died; now there was not a breath of wind. The line they had been hunting had run, before hounds turned right-handed, roughly in a southerly direction. So he would have walked north, towards the pole-star, the general direction of kennels and his three-roomed house in the stable-yard, his home. *If* the pole-star had been out.

He took a few steps, rather aimlessly, and saw, to his glad surprise, a country road. A road, like a river, is likely to lead to some habitation, so he began to walk along the road in the direction he had been facing. He did not limp, he felt no pain or hurt of any kind. Still not believing, fearing that somehow he must have been mistaken, he put his right hand up to his eyes, to his face again. No blood, no cut or wound that he could feel; he had not been mistaken.

He walked on. He walked on, not thinking much of anything, just kept on walking. He must have walked, a good two miles, but no car came by, nothing came, from either direction. He did not know what to do but keep on the way he was going, though it might be north, south, east, or west, for all he knew. It was not something he would choose to do, walk a rough, rutty road in top-boots that fitted him, now, too well—for it must be admitted that the huntsman was somewhat vain, when he could afford it, in the matter of such things as hunting livery, military uniforms, formal dress— Suddenly he thought of something:

He stopped, pulled the hunting horn from between the buttons of his coat, and, pressing the horn to his lips, blew. He blew the long, rising, falling call he used for calling a lost hound. As the last note died, he felt rather foolish—standing there in the road, child-like, blowing a horn. Still, it could do no harm; there seemed to be no one to

rouse. It was like shooting off a gun when you were
lost in the woods. Someone might hear; someone
might answer. Recklessly, he blew again.

As he took the horn from his lips, he thought, for
an instant, that he was hearing an echo; who else in
the country would be blowing a hunting horn? The
master carried a horn in a case on his saddle, having
arranged a set of signals with the huntsman in case
they should be some distance apart; one was "Let's

call it a day." But the master blew his horn on only one occasion: the horn was not an honest hunting horn but had a reed, and it gave out a thin, emasculated note, highly ludicrous, which, on this one and only occasion, the huntsman did not happen to hear —only heard about it afterwards.

Oh, nothing like the horn the huntsman heard now! For this was not an echo. Someone else was blowing—someone that really knew how to blow. The huntsman listened with delight. A high, clear, flawlessly pure note—far beyond the huntsman's capacity. But—he would swear—not on any short copper hunting horn. Not *that* music. Ah, someone was mocking him, showing him up!—and, ashamed, he tucked his horn away. . . . But, as he stood listening to the other horn, he knew, somehow, that it was not mockery although the call was indeed something like the one he himself had just blown, only more beautiful, more insistent, more compelling. "Come away—ee . . . away—ee . . . away—ee" it seemed to say, and that was what it meant. Come along in, come along home, the day is done— come away! What poor lost hound would not leave a line that must be hunted no longer and come along home, when he heard that call? . . . The music died away. But it had come from the general direction in which the huntsman had been walking, and so, much puzzled, he continued on his way.

He walked on and on, and it seemed to him that he had walked many miles, and still no car passed, though the evening was still young; and no house or barn or building of any kind appeared along the road. The road, so far as he could judge in the dark, still ran fairly straight in the direction of the horn-blowing, and since *someone* must have blown the horn, it seemed best to keep on going the way he was. But he was terribly tired from the long, hard day in the saddle and the long trek on the country road, and his feet, in boots meant for riding only, were fast becoming an agony. This road, of course, might run on for twenty or thirty miles in a back country—and this was probably that type of country —and not lead past any habitation and finally end up—as it must, sometime—in a strange town or village; but whether he could last that long, he wasn't at all sure. He plodded on along the hard,

43

rutted road and presently he became really discouraged, he was losing hope, when all of a sudden he saw, some distance ahead and close to the side of the road, a light. He thanked Heaven—he felt like kneeling down there in the road and offering thanks to God, the way pious people do when thrown up on a safe beach after a shipwreck. And now, seeing the light, seeing that it was a lighted house by the side of the road, and knowing he could get help and that somehow they would find hounds and get them back to kennels—though that might not be easy, might even take days—he was ashamed that a few minutes before he had been so close to damning everything and railing at the hellish time—as he had begun to regard it—he was going through: the utter weariness, the torture of putting foot to ground, the despair of finding anybody, any human creature, that night. For—when he remembered the mantrap he had run into—he was really lucky. It might have been so much worse. Suppose in that crashing fall—but had there been a fall? and he put his hand up to his eyes and face again—suppose he had broken his back or his pelvis, or even a leg, and so had been unable to move? He might have lain there all that night—but no, the girl would have come back and found him—and that would have further complicated things. He was lucky that he had not been badly hurt—he had not been hurt at all, which was a miracle—and that he had been able to get up and walk and, in the end, find a house, a lighted house.

There were several lights, he saw, as he turned in at the driveway. Curtains were drawn across the windows of lighted rooms, all was quiet, no car stood in the cobblestone drive, and yet there was the air of a party going on. And the huntsman saw at once, even in the dark, that this was no bare, stark farmhouse, such as one might expect to find in a back country. From what he could make out, it was a small house of two storeys, somewhat spread-out for its size—the kind of house he would like to have had. In a country he once knew when he was a boy, where he had grown up on hunting and where, perhaps, he had been happiest, there had been many houses such as this; little houses that could honestly be called hunting-boxes, since they had been built in a hunting country, so-called,

45

and were actually quite small. But in many hunting countries hunting-boxes were, more often than not, imposing mansions.

Finding no bell, but there being a brass knocker on the door, the huntsman let the striking part fall gently so as not to make too loud a knock. Almost at once the door opened—someone must have been standing on the other side.

"Come in, Mr. Huntsman," a courteous voice said. "We have been expecting you."

Now, if we put ourselves in the huntsman's place, we must remember that he was, at the moment, close to the point of exhaustion, that he had been in the saddle since eleven that morning to four in the afternoon, that he had had a bad fall—if the fall had been a dream, then all was but a dream— and that he had walked . . . well, some six or seven miles on a rough, dirt road, and that he had had no food or drink since an early breakfast, except for a sandwich and a swallow of sherry. So, when the door opened and a voice at once called him by name, or, anyway, by his professional title, and especially when he saw the strange, fantastic figure

that faced him in the rather dim light of the
vestibule, no wonder he felt that he was entering
another dream world, less real, even, than the one
he had just left, where he had found himself un-
marked, apparently, by the wire, unhurt after that
shattering fall. . . .

But this is my old hunt, was the huntsman's first
thought, for the short, lean, bearded figure at the

open door was dressed in a scarlet full-dress evening coat with the yellow lapels and the black velvet collar the huntsman knew so well. Before my time, thought the huntsman, for he had never seen this little ginger-coloured gentleman before—and then, struck dumb, the huntsman saw the black silk knee-breeches, the black silk stockings, and pumps with silver buckles. This chap had really done the thing in a big way; no one, in the huntsman's day, had ever dared go quite so far.

"Thank you," the huntsman said, stepping over the threshold.

"You are a little late," the other said. He shut the door, looking up at the huntsman, smiling, showing very white, rather fierce-looking teeth. His reddish beard was carefully trimmed to a fine point; his moustache had an upward sweep. "We waited and waited," he said in his polite way, "and then we went ahead. But we saved something for you."

"Thank you," said the huntsman again, wondering what it was all about, trying to recall if he had accepted a dinner invitation, and then knowing of course he had not. He said, "Now, if I could use your phone—I must telephone kennels. My hounds got away——"

"Everything is taken care of," the figure in scarlet interrupted him. "Your first whip stopped them, just before dark. Aided by your young lady, I might add. They're safe in kennels now."

The huntsman stared at him. "But—but—how—how d'you——"

"How do we know?" the other finished it for him. "Oh," he said gaily, "we have so many little birds here."

Very facetious, the huntsman thought. He did not feel at all that way. "There's also a loose horse," he began stiffly.

"Your aged friend?" the other asked, smiling. "We have him in our stable. You see? There's nothing in the world to worry about."

"Is he . . ." the huntsman hesitated. "Is he all right?"

"He's perfectly all right," the other said, suddenly serious; "now." He took the huntsman's arm and steered him towards a flight of stairs leading to the floor above. "Fed and watered—or, I should say, beered; he drank half a bucket of beer," he explained. "Your room's the second——"

"And by the way," the huntsman said, to put things straight, "the young lady you speak of is not 'my young lady.' If any——"

"Is it even so?" The little chap in scarlet looked up at him in a mocking way.

"If any little bird told you *that*," the huntsman said, smiling, "you can——"

"They're great gossips, of course," the other said; "especially the sparrows. The story was you might bring her along with you this evening. We'd have managed a"—he paused—"a hen party for *her*; this, of course, is a strictly stag affair." He stopped and looked up at the huntsman. "For a very good reason, which you will soon understand."

But the huntsman was thinking of something else. "She helped stop hounds, did she? Well, good for her! I sent her to the right place, then, after all."

"The right place?" the other repeated, giving the huntsman a strange look. "Well. . . ." Then, abruptly he left this, and said, "Your room's the

50

second on the right. You'll want a bath and a change. D'you mind a white tie? It's rather an occasion, you see."

"But I have no evening clothes——"

"But they were *made* for you," the other said gaily. "Come down as soon as you can. The dining-room's in there." He nodded at a closed door beyond the stairs. "We'll be still at table—these chaps sit forever over their port."

"A bootjack?" the huntsman said, hesitantly. "Could I borrow——?"

"This is a *hunting* country, Mr. Huntsman. There's a bootjack in every room."

The huntsman smiled. As he turned to mount the stairs, he said, "I recognize your colours. You must have been a member before I came. I used to hunt hounds in that country."

Smiling, the little gingery chap looked up at him. "I am tempted," he said, "to a slang expression I never liked: 'Are *you* telling me?'" He threw back his head and laughed, so infectiously that the huntsman began to laugh too, though why he could not say. "Do you remember," the other asked, "the

51

great January run, over Mount Mercy, beyond the
Fishing Dam?"

"*Do* I?" the huntsman broke in. "Why, there
never *was* such a run—except today."

"Oh, come now!" The other's face fell.

"Of course," the huntsman hastened to add, "that
Mount Mercy run we accounted for our fox."

"You did indeed."

"You were along that day?" the huntsman asked
politely, but he thought perhaps this little chap was
one of those cheerful liars that jump those five-foot
fences and have all those tremendous adventures
when no one else is there. For the huntsman knew

the Mount Mercy run by heart—it was during his huntsmanship—and he could name everyone—there were not many—in the field that day. "The kill was just beyond Crabtree Run. You were there?" He made it scarcely a question, said it in a perfunctory way, still very polite, as one stating an obvious fact.

"Yes." Still smiling his rather fixed smile, the chap in scarlet gazed straight at the huntsman, and such was the look in his eyes, so open, fearless, and, at the same time, gentle, that the huntsman must believe, even though he could swear that the truth was the other way. "Yes," the little chap said again; "I was there." He gave the huntsman a kindly pat in the small of the back. "Now run along."

The huntsman went up the stairs and into the second room on the right. Lights were turned on in the room and a little fire was burning in the fire-place, but what caught his eye first was a scarlet full-dress evening coat with the facings and collar of his present hunt; this was hung over the back of a chair, and across the chair's seat were the braided evening trousers—not knee-breeches, to his relief, for he was a conservative man—and, on the rug

53

beside the chair, a pair of patent leather evening shoes with trees. Laid out on the bed were a white starched shirt, studded and cuff-linked; a white waistcoat with the hunt's brass—or gold, perhaps—buttons; collar, white tie, folded white handkerchief —the full equipment. A mahogany bootjack with handle bar stood up on its own feet near the fire-place.

The huntsman stood motionless for a moment, gazing at the scarlet evening coat, and suddenly—perhaps because he was so weary and so confused as to what had happened to him, and what was now happening—suddenly he felt the tears smarting in his eyes and he had to swallow hard. Such a small, unimportant thing—but he had never in his life owned a scarlet evening coat. Now, in a hunting country the first thing, generally, the gentlemen that are entitled to wear pink, or scarlet, in the field do is to buy—since all is vanity—a pink, or scarlet, evening coat, and this is generally worn at all formal evening parties during the hunting season. Such a coat, with its brass, or gold, buttons engraved with the hunt's initials or device or even of more

54

elaborate design, with its dyed silk facings and velvet
collar of the hunt's colours, is fearfully expensive,
and the huntsman, before he *was* a professional
huntsman, never felt he could rightly spend all that
money on, after all, a kind of fancy dress. Even in
the hunting field—when he was simply a member
of the field—he did not wear scarlet, though urged
to, but an old-fashioned, long black coat that had
belonged to his father, a coat so stiff and weathered
that, like a suit of armour, it could almost stand
up of itself. Now—and when he had served as
whipper-in—his livery for the field—scarlet coat,

white breeches, velvet cap, and the rest—was provided by the hunt. But, of course, no evening dress, and, anyway, the huntsman held that a professional, a hunt servant—which was what he was—should not wear the scarlet evening coat—though people would have told him his case was different—and so he had never owned one. And now. . . . He stood gazing at the beautiful garment—"made for you," his host downstairs had said. Well, anything was possible, *this* evening. . . . And he felt, even with the childish tears in his eyes, suddenly quite happy. . . .

Now bathed and groomed, and dressed to the eyes in the perfectly fitting scarlet swallow-tail, the huntsman opened the door to the dining-room and saw, in the light of many candelabra, what he might already have guessed—that he had chanced—*chanced?*—upon a hunt dinner. The room was ablaze with scarlet. Some twenty figures in scarlet coats—about ten couple, he would say at a glance, as he would say in counting hounds—sat at a long mahogany table from which the cloth had been drawn. And then he saw—and in that instant his heart seemed to contract and he felt a numbing fear as in beholding some supernatural thing—he saw— his eyes swept round the table again—yes, each figure wore a pointed, reddish beard—like that worn by the one who had opened the front door. *They all looked alike*—that was the strange, terrifying thing. . . .

All talk died as the huntsman entered, and now a chair was pushed back at the other end of the table from the door, and one of the scarlet-clad figures came to meet him, and when the courteous voice said again, "Come in, Mr. Huntsman," he recognized him whom he thought of as his host—the one that had opened the front door. For there was, indeed, scarcely any way to tell one from another, except, perhaps by their voices, their manner of speaking, by one's having a beard a little greyer, more grizzled than the figure on his right or left. And then the huntsman saw, too, that besides the uniformity of the scarlet, each coat had the yellow facings and black collar of the huntsman's old hunt. And it broke upon him then—dazed and confused as he was, taking part in some crazy dream—that the whole thing was a joke, an elaborate, practical joke, with false beards, or masks, perhaps, and that these were all men he knew, members of his old hunt, and that in a moment or two the beards, or the masks, would be taken off. . . .

"This way, Mr. Huntsman," his host said, and led the huntsman, behind the backs of the chairs, along one side to the head of the table. Talk had been quickly resumed and, politely, everyone avoided looking at the huntsman who had arrived so late and was, at the moment, so conspicuous.

"This is your place, Mr. Huntsman." His host indicated an empty chair, the seat of the most honoured guest, at the right of the head of the table. Another scarlet-coated figure, wearing silk knee-breeches—exactly like all the rest, the huntsman presumed—pulled back the chair.

"Thank you," said the huntsman to him, for the latter, dressed as he was, was obviously not a butler or footman—not even a hunt servant, the huntsman thought, smiling to himself. He was somewhat taken aback at this extreme courtesy. His host, standing behind the chair at the head of the table, waited for

the huntsman to take his seat; his host, then, was the
owner of the house, or the toastmaster of the dinner
—or the master of the hunt—another hunt, though
the colours were the same. . . . For the huntsman
saw now that the face was not a mask and that the
beard was not false and that this was no one he had
ever known.

A place had been set for him on the dark, gleaming board. He unfolded his napkin and sat staring
down at the empty plate with intense concentration
as the voices rose about him. A plate of clear soup
was set before him and then at once his sherry glass
—one of four wine-glasses, he counted—was filled.
Both arms that served him had scarlet sleeves, and
turning slightly in his chair, he saw that he was
being waited on by two of the scarlet-clad figures.
Embarrassed, he looked at his host.

"Am I so awfully late?" he apologized, meaning,
so late that the servants had been let go and that
now two of the guests were taking their places.

"Not at all," his host said. "It is one of our cus-
toms. We call them 'Apprentices,' " he exclaimed.
"They *serve* a certain term"—he smiled at the mild

joke—"before being admitted to full privileges—*and obligations.*"

"What a good idea!" said the huntsman politely. "Solves the servant problem . . . I hear so much about," he added, to dispel any thought that he might have such a problem.

"The servant problem," his host said, not in surprise, not making it a question. He might have been recalling something out of the past. He looked at the huntsman and said in his

gentle, courteous voice, "We are all servants here."

The huntsman was not embarrassed; he believed him. Now this was a strange thing, for it was the kind of remark one doesn't generally hear at a dinner party; much less at a stag affair such as this, held in celebration of what many people regard as one of the cruellest of blood sports. Any other time, the huntsman would have put it down as sententious and smug and stuffy in the extreme, and, with a polite murmur of agreement, gone on to something less ponderous. But he did not have that feeling. No, it seemed to him that the little bearded chap, dressed as he was and, evidently, a killer along with the rest of them, had spoken in all sincerity; that he was sustained by an inner spirit, a belief, a conviction—the huntsman was not sure of the right word—something, anyway, that he himself had never known.

"Well, Mr. Huntsman," his host said in a different tone of voice and with a slight note of raillery, "you came to the horn, didn't you?"

The huntsman nodded, smiling at the other's use of hunting parlance. "Actually," he replied, "I was on my way here—I mean I was always headed in the right direction."

His host smiled too, showing his fine teeth, of which he may have been justly proud. "Yes," he said gravely, "I think you may say that, Mr. Huntsman."

"I beg your pardon?"

"That you were always headed in the right direction."

The huntsman, not quite sure what the other

meant, picked up his sherry glass and drank. He knew little about wine, he was not much of a wine drinker, or a drinker of any kind—his job was too demanding and strenuous—but he knew when he sipped the sherry that this was something special —just as the clear soup he was now drinking was the best he had ever tasted. Yes, these chaps really did themselves well. They were busy with the port now—and he saw, to his surprise, that the decanters were being sent round the table against the course of the sun—as the phrase was—counter-clockwise, and, in a way, this seemed the strangest thing of all. To the huntsman, it was like finding himself suddenly transported, without sea trip or flight, to a country where the rule of the road was different.

He said now, as an Apprentice removed the empty soup-plate and put in its stead what the huntsman saw was the fish course, "I meant to say—I meant to ask you about that horn. I've heard some of the best"—he forbore from putting in that he himself had won first prize for horn-blowing in a not very large horse show—"but the chap who blew me home"—he corrected himself—"blew me here to-night——"

"Blew you *home*," his host interrupted him in a firm voice. "That is quite right, Mr. Huntsman; you must learn to think of it"—he made a sweeping gesture to include the room, the house, perhaps this far country itself—"as home."

"You are very kind," murmured the huntsman, accepting it as the kind of excessively hospitable remark one makes when the wine flows freely.

"Yes," his host went on, after a moment's silence.

"He's one of our best horn-blowers . . . but I think it only fair to tell you that he uses a trumpet rather than one of your little hunting horns."

"I thought so," said the huntsman.

"Yes," the other said, "*we* think that some day he'll . . . how shall I put it? . . . well, receive almost universal recognition."

"I should certainly think so," said the huntsman politely. An Apprentice filled one of the huntsman's glasses with a pale, still, yellow wine. The huntsman had emptied the sherry glass. Now he sipped the chilled, dry white wine, and he wondered from what famed vineyard, of what great year? Already he was feeling a little light-headed, from the long hunt, the long, long walk on the road. . . . "I was wondering," he said, turning to his host, "where the road led to. I was quite lost, in a strange country. To some village or town, I suppose. . . ."

"Eventually, of course, to the city," his host replied. The huntsman waited, but the other did not name the city, and the huntsman was ashamed to ask, ashamed of his ignorance.

"I'm glad I landed here," the huntsman said.

"What would they have thought—my turning up in the city, in a red coat, on foot——"

"The Marines would have stopped you," said the other laughing, "along one of the purple streets." Confused, the huntsman stared at him. The other went on, "Some P.F.C. from a green mountain who never heard of *your* kind of hunting would think one of Cornwallis's lobsters was on the loose."

His host was choosing to be obscure. One thing the huntsman did understand. "The Marines?" he repeated. "Troops, you mean. Sounds like martial law——"

"Oh, there's nothing to worry about," the other broke in. "Here, the situation has always been well in hand. But it's a duty those soldiers of the sea always wanted, and—I might add—one they were pretty sure they'd get. Perhaps that was one reason why they were always being pushed around. But who could refuse them? Surely, they were about due for a soft job after all the hard ones they had."

The huntsman tried to stop an Apprentice from filling another glass with red wine. The white wine had not kept pace with the fish course, which was

66

gone, and now the meat was before him. The huntsman's gesture was insincere and feeble: he managed to stop the Apprentice just as the red wine reached a proper height in the glass. The huntsman was now feeling in top form, but he remembered the cost (for never could he stand much to drink) and as he tasted the dark, rich, heady draught, he turned to his host and said:

"I shall pay for all this in the morning, I know, but one doesn't often meet with such wines; at least, *I* don't——"

"That has been corrected," his host interrupted him again. "You may proceed with impunity—up to a certain point, which you will soon learn to recognize. Me, when I find myself telling how I beat Eliza, one of the best of the bitch pack—before your time—over the ice, then I know I've reached what we may call the saturation point."

"I know," the huntsman said, somewhat puzzled at this last statement, but anxious, for his part, to confide in this delightful chap. "On occasions, I have the most tremendous desire to sing close harmony. Then *I* know; for I'm really very bad

67

with music. But I should have to be fairly tight for that. As a matter of fact, I do feel at this moment that I'm not so far off from wanting to join in in . . . oh, 'Drink puppy, drink' or 'D'ye ken John Peel' or——"

The other threw back his head and burst out laughing. "What contempt we used to have for those lays!" he exclaimed. "I remember standing on the hill one night in the moonlight, and I remember the house below—with a dinner much like this going on—the house all lit up—and the guests the same— and those awful songs, all off key. . . ." He paused,

and then, smiling, looked at the huntsman and said in his kindly way, "They're very fine songs, really. Now, of course, we understand."

But the huntsman was all confusion again: What was his host doing up on a hill in the moonlight? One of those Southern night-hunters? Was that it? A farmer—or a moonshiner, perhaps. . . . And what about this question of drink? "You mean," the huntsman asked, and he touched his glass of red wine, "that this is . . . well, that this, and all the rest, won't—er—won't give one a head in the morning?"

"The unduly heavy penalty," his host began, taking a sip of port and giving his moustache a brush upwards, "prescribed for . . . well, for merely a modest binge if I may so put it, was conceded to be a mistake. Unfortunately, once the rules had been formulated, involving, as they did, certain chemical actions and reactions, nothing could be done about it at the lower level, as we say in government circles. It was, as you may imagine, engineered by a strong and aggressive minority. Of course, once you get beyond the finite order"—he made a wide gesture with his right arm—"all that can be changed. You will understand that, I am sure."

The huntsman was not sure he did. Certainly, it was against all the rules *he* knew. He tried to put his thought in words: "Somehow, it doesn't seem quite fair. What I mean is, that I should go through all these"—he indicated the array of wine-glasses—"and wake up feeling like a—like a——"

"Lark," the other supplied; "the bird, I mean. One of our favourites. There's one always around. Yes," he went on, after a moment, "it was agreed among the higher-ups—if you understand me—that a constant and cordial relationship with certain products of the grape *and* the grain should not entail the morning-after malaise, lassitude, distaste for all nourishment . . . that is to say, the usual punishment was conceded to be unduly cruel, and the whole thing was, so to speak, declared unconstitutional— as affecting the higher level, that is."

" 'The higher level'?" the huntsman repeated, confused at what he considered an annoying double-talk.

"In other words," said the other, laughing, "there *is* pie in the sky. Yes, Mr. Huntsman, I guarantee that you will be joining the lark in a duet in the morning . . . however"—and he pointed to the huntsman's fourth glass, which had not yet been filled—"it might be well for you to take the bubbles out of the champagne."

The huntsman thought that when it came to the champagne he would forego *that*, and he glanced round the table to see how the others were doing with their port, and suddenly he saw something, or, rather, someone he had not noticed before: this was a figure, sitting back a little from the table and partly hidden by the companions on his left and right, and he wore, instead of the scarlet coat of all the rest, a coat of light grey—with orange facings, the huntsman saw, not yellow, and a dark brown, instead of a black, collar. A visitor, evidently, from another hunt, he looked leaner . . . yes, actually less well-nourished than the others. He had not their bold, assertive look, and perhaps that was the reason the huntsman had not noticed him earlier.

Curious, he turned to his host. "I don't want to appear inquisitive," he said, diffidently, "but your friend in the grey coat . . . I've never seen

71

that before. Is he . . .?" the huntsman hesitated.

"Not one of ours, as you see," his host replied—
rather shortly, the huntsman thought. "He comes
from another country—a country, by the way, that
we finally gave up. Sour grapes, of course," he said,
giving the huntsman a meaning look. "But . . ."
and here he paused in the manner of one about to
get off something good, "we never did move in his
circles."

The huntsman laughed dutifully, hollowly—the

way one laughs when he knows a joke has been made but does not see it. He thought he was getting a little dense from all the wine he had drunk—despite what his host had said about impunity—and he was casting about in his mind for a new subject, when the other leaned towards him and, fixing him with his tawny, yellowish eyes, said slowly, significantly:

"Actually, he asked himself, when he heard you were coming."

"Oh, no thanks," said the huntsman, putting his hand out and preventing the Apprentice from filling the champagne glass quite up to the brim. "What was that?" he said, but he had heard every word. "I never saw him before," he said, glancing down the table at the figure in grey.

"That will come later," his host said in a calm, level voice.

When one of the decanters of port came round to him—the wrong way, of course, but that seemed to be their rule here, like driving on the left of the road —the huntsman did not take the stopper out but slid the heavy decanter along the mahogany to his right.

"Aha!" said the latter, giving the huntsman a look. "Close to close harmony, what?"

"Oh, very good!" the huntsman said, laughing loudly, knowing, of course, underneath the layers of sherry, Chablis, Burgundy, champagne, and, now, port, that it was nothing to roar with laughter at. But he had a feeling, closer to unmanning fear than he had ever known, that he must be terribly agreeable now; that these people were against him, for some reason, and that he must do everything he could to placate them. And yet the little chap on his other side, his right, seemed friendly enough. He had been rather silent at first, but that, of course, was to let the huntsman finish his dinner undisturbed. Now he began to talk.

"New Year's Day at Greenhill?" repeated the huntsman in answer to a question from him. "Yes, I remember: we only hunted that country once, in my time. Very short run, that day."

"Fortunately! You had all been up till dawn——"

"Not I——"

"Well, most of the field had. I always say, you can't mix alcohol and——"

"Petrol."

"Not our dish, of course. No, I meant hunting. On the lower level, that is." (Damn all this lower and higher level stuff! thought the huntsman.) "Too much bubbly water," the other went on, "the night before. Why, I saw five refusals at a three-foot post and rails: my good friends the horses knew what was wrong.

"I suppose," he said, after a moment, "you might expect an apology from the enemy for putting up such a poor show—forty-three minutes, to be exact."

"You've got a good memory," the huntsman said. He couldn't remember the time of that run, but he was sure the other was right.

"It's the sort of thing one doesn't forget," said the other, with a peculiar smile. "Well, to be fair, the enemy was not up to snuff. He'd been having a bit of a moonlight celebration himself the night before, big chicken dinner and——"

"And moonshine whisky, I suppose," the huntsman put in, smiling, trying to please. Who *were* these people, anyway? His neighbour said, "The enemy rather counted on New Year's Day being like Christmas, or Easter—holy days, days of peace."

"I'm afraid war doesn't wait on holy days," the huntsman said soberly.

"That's true. Not any more, anyway. Damn' little of that sort of thing left. . . ."

This was the kind of talk that went on round the table—the kind you'd hear at any hunt dinner; about this tremendous run and that—all a deadly bore unless you yourself had been there. These dinners—so the huntsman had observed in his time —could be quite a different thing from dinners held in celebration of other sports, such as yachting or football, for example. Fox hunting was a blood sport, and the huntsman used to wonder sometimes if the presence of that element and the ever-present chance of injury or death to its followers could account for the peculiar behaviour of its celebrants. The men that devoted a large part of their lives to hunting—and by hunting he meant riding to hounds for the purpose of killing the fox, the stag, or the hare or of simply following a bag of aniseed or other artificial quarry dragged across country—hunting men, as they were sometimes called—and a few

women he had known—were more rapt, more fanatical, than other sportsmen, and their lives were, sometimes, terribly limited. The huntsman, who found time, though not much, for other interests, other pursuits, thought of these men as belonging to a peculiar order, devoted to one certain purpose—to kill. And now, this night, going back in his mind over the years he had spent with people of this kind, this dinner tonight and these scarlet-clad, fierce-eyed little chaps reminded him, in a way, of the mess of a fighter-pilot squadron on active duty. Death was not here so wholesale, but, as had been remarked, the grave was always open.

Well, wars would go on, he supposed, but the sport of fox hunting was, perhaps, on the way out. And suddenly it struck him that he was thinking of his hunting days—his very life, then—as being over and done with, and this was a strange thing to be thinking, for hunting would probably last as long as he did, and he put the thought out of his mind. For, he told himself, the pack was safely kennelled— thanks partly to that girl—and they would all go a-hunting—the day after tomorrow.

"You spoke of that young lady," he heard himself say to his host, and he knew he should not have gone in for the strong, full-bodied port after all the rest.

"I'm sorry. . . ." The host bent his head towards the huntsman; the table was getting noisier.

"The girl who helped the whip stop hounds."

"Oh, yes. Certainly. What about her?"

"Nothing," said the huntsman, thinking better of it. "Except . . ."

"Except what?"

"She ought to get rid of that horse," the huntsman said, and felt the anger rising in him.

"Why, Mr. Huntsman . . ." his host began, teasingly.

"I'm thinking of hounds," the huntsman said. "I don't want my hounds overridden."

"Aren't you thinking of her, too?" the other asked, and he was deadly serious now.

"I'm thinking of the rest of the field," the huntsman said, like a small boy, persisting. "The horse is a menace—crossing people at fences—she can't hold him——"

"But aren't you thinking of *her*—first of all?"

"Naturally I don't want to see her hurt," the huntsman said gruffly. "You see," he said, deciding suddenly to confide in his host, "she's really not very good with a horse. She never will be, I'm afraid."

"She never will be," the other repeated; "but I am not afraid."

The huntsman looked at him. But his host went on quickly, now in a teasing way again, "Of course, that would hold no appeal for you."

"What did you say?" Everybody seemed to be talking at once.

"Wouldn't you find it strange, Mr. Huntsman,"

79

the other asked, smiling at him, "to find yourself falling for a girl who couldn't tell one bay horse from another?"

" 'Falling'?" repeated the huntsman in astonishment. "Me? I'm afraid," he said scornfully, "that one of your little birds gave you the wrong steer there."

"I think not."

"You're imagining things——"

"*You* never would, Mr. Huntsman."

"Not that, certainly," said the huntsman firmly. "In the first place, the thing would be impossible——"

"In the first place, yes," said the other, looking full at the huntsman; "but in *last* place?"

The huntsman did not attempt to answer. He put the remark down as one of those too profound to inquire into or as a bogus epigram made more for the sound, the contrast, of the words, rather than for any real meaning. He fell silent and, turning the empty wine-glass in his fingers, listened to the high-pitched voices around him. They spoke a strange language, but the huntsman understood most of it, and he sat there, and now the thing began swiftly to unfold, to assume a dreadful clarity.

80

"Foil—foil. . . . Ranger's Brook—yes, but damned cold on the feet——" "Better than burnt-over fields, still smoking——" "The hot-foot, you might say." "Tied up in a bag—your uncle, really?" "Damned humiliating——" "A bagman, they call 'em in the old country; sounds *so* underprivileged——" "Rioted on a duck, I give you my word——" "Oh, a point of ten kilometres——"

The huntsman turned his head sharply. He did not hear the rest. He said in a low voice to his host, "Someone said 'kilometres'? I heard the word distinctly." He felt the fear coming back on him. "Where——" he began and was about to say, "Where *are we*?" but he could not bring himself to ask—he was afraid.

"Oh, yes," his host said carelessly. "We use the metric system. We think it better." He smiled. "We believe in retaining the best features of each."

"I notice," the huntsman said, and, so help him, he could not keep his voice steady, "that you send the port round the table the opposite way—that is, counter-clockwise—against the sun, as some would say. . . ."

The other was looking at him, smiling, showing his white, beautiful teeth through the red beard. " 'Against the sun'?" he repeated. "But, Mr. Huntsman," he said in high, triumphant voice, "doesn't that depend on where you are?"

"Of course," the huntsman said; "yes, of course." He tore his eyes away from the other's steady gaze. Round about him the voices went on:

"So they started digging——"

"Sent back to kennels for the terrier, I understand?"

"Yes, I gave little Jonesy one he didn't soon forget. . . ."

The huntsman found himself staring across the table at the figure that had just spoken—one of the older, more grizzled sportsmen. The latter may have sensed the huntsman's intense gaze, for he turned from the companion on his left and looked at the huntsman.

"Yes," he said, and it seemed to be for the huntsman he was speaking. "I had nothing against young Mr. Jones, but I was naturally annoyed when they brought *him* into the picture. This was something new; they'd never gone in for *that* refinement before." Here he leaned across the table and spoke directly to the huntsman: "You can confirm me in that, sir."

So it *is* a dream, the huntsman thought, and tried to wrench himself awake, out of the fear, the horror —the way one does sometimes when a dream can no longer be borne. But he did not come awake. And now he realized that all the others at the long table were quiet; were hanging on the words of the figure that had just spoken.

"Young Mr. Jones," the speaker went on, "came fast and straight down the corridor—of course that's what the terrier breeds are so proud of: take on anything. Stupid, we used to think. But each must have his pride. . . . As I say, I had nothing against Jonesy. I'd seen him and his brothers and sisters—from quite close, too, for there was no danger of gun powder in *your* country, sir"—and he gave the huntsman a little formal bow—"playing around the kennels, they were, and they *were* such a gay, lively lot, I took quite a fancy to them. But this little Jones was asking for trouble, and for a moment or two I thought seriously of sending him along ahead of me. For, of course, I saw then," he added in a matter-of-fact way, "that the game was up—as we used to say."

He paused to refill his glass from one of the decanters of port, which had reached him some moments before. The huntsman sat there in stricken silence. And then the other did an unexpected thing: he leaned across the table, seized the huntsman's glass, which had stood empty now for some time, drew it towards him and filled it from the decanter.

"Oh, no thanks," the huntsman said in a strange, cracked voice. He made a long arm in vain protest. The other slid the filled glass across the table to him.

"You'd better have a drop," he said, kindly. "You've had a long day of it."

The huntsman, blindly obeying, started to raise his glass, but he saw that his hand was actually trembling, so he left the glass there on the table. No one noticed—or if any did, they showed no sign.

"You see," the story-teller went on cheerfully, "I was no longer young, and what with the shovels and spades and picks and mattocks *and* Mr. Jones, they meant to have an end of it, one way or another. Yes, I could have sent young Jonesy on ahead of me, down there in the darkness, but, instead, I let him have one or two to teach him not to be so cocky, but nothing really serious, for he was a young chap with a brilliant future—as it turned out—and he came of such a nice little family."

At this, a great roar of laughter went up, and while the table rocked, the huntsman picked up his glass, with steadier hand now, and swallowed some of the strong wine.

"So," the story-teller said when the laughter subsided, "I simply bolted . . . which, as you know"—and he looked at the huntsman—"is a way we have. You were kind enough," he added, speaking directly to the huntsman, "to allow five minutes' law. However, it was not enough—that day—you may remember."

Yes, the huntsman remembered. He remembered this chap . . . and he would remember the others, all the others there, should they care to identify themselves to him. He knew who they were now, and as he glanced round the table in a kind of horror, the scarlet ones, the bearded faces, these dread figures, seemed to press closer and closer, and he tried, he tried, with awful desperation, to blot out the room, the faces, the masks, all this thing, and to burst into the real world. . . .

"There is nothing to fear, Mr. Huntsman," he heard his host say. "And there is nothing to regret." He spoke in the cool, measured voice of authority, and all the table listened. The huntsman sat with lowered head, endlessly twisting the stem of his wine-glass round and round in his fingers. He heard one of the heavy decanters being slid along the gleaming board; for a moment there was no other sound. Then his host began to speak, and it was a little like an after-dinner speech—though he did not rise—in that it had a certain formal ring and seemed to be addressed to the whole room.

"Once, without ever being sought, life was thrust upon us all, and to live, one must eat, and to eat, one must kill and, yes, one must sometimes steal. And once, in the old, old days it was a kind of game—rough, to be sure; no quarter asked or given—but fair enough, fair enough. . . . And then later"—here he turned his head and spoke to the huntsman—"later you asked yourselves, Why should we be fair to the thief of the world? and so instead of depending on the nose and speed and power of one, you packed together hundreds of villainous dogs——"

"Hounds," someone said, laughing at the speaker's vehemence.

"I'm sorry—hounds." The speaker smiled and went on, more mildly: "And they sent to the ends of the earth for the blood of swifter horses, and they sent men out at night when all decent folk were *not* home and *out* of bed" (laughter) "to barricade those same homes against the decent folk's finding sanctuary——"

The huntsman looked up—turned to him. "We never stopped earths in our country," he said quietly.

"You alone are not on trial, Mr. Huntsman," the speaker said. "It is so-called civilization."

"Hear, hear!" several cried out, laughing.

"They used spades and shovels and pickaxes and crowbars to tear up these homes and so to evict these decent folk. They imported specialists in the underground—otherwise known as terriers" (more laughter). . . . "Manœuvres," he went on, when they were quiet again, "manœuvres, tricks, gadgets— all to catch the poor thief of the world!" He gave a little scornful laugh, and then in a voice several notes lower and in an organ-like tone, said, "All to destroy these same decent folk."

"Hear! Hear!"

"Splendid form he's in tonight, isn't he?" the huntsman's neighbour on his right whispered. The huntsman, who was not impervious to the orator's art, gulped down the last of his wine.

"Once," the speaker went on, slowly, spacing his words, "regarded by these same decent folk as mean, dastardly, but now"—here he returned to his earlier, lighter manner—"well, fair enough—not too unfair. . . .

"Not too unfair," he repeated, and now he was

playing another movement, gayer, almost dance-like, "to be bundled into a sack, like the uncle of our friend here, and dropped in some dark cover——"

"Who was it," one of them interrupted, "who was tied up in a sack and thrown into the Seine, or was it the sea?"

"*Better a cover than the river*," someone sang out, as if in answer to a cue.

It was a song familiar to all there evidently, for now all joined in, in tremendous voice:

"Better a cover than the river,
Better a brief hour, clear and free—
Even the heart-break over the stubble—
Better a spinney than the sea."

The host held up his hand. "So we all thought," he said, smiling; "once.

"Not too unfair," he went on, spinning out the theme, "to send a whip to sink the wind"—he gave the huntsman a sly glance—"or even to send a pretty girl to get a view." But the huntsman did not rise to it; he sat there with bowed head, twisting the stem of his empty glass. There was a short silence. Then the speaker, in a different voice and speaking directly to the huntsman, said with great seriousness:

"Mr. Huntsman. So far as our members are concerned, you have played the game fair and square. We have not one single charge to make, not one fault to find. A just man, a loyal friend, a fair foe, you are our dear guest tonight. What more can I say—for us?

"*But*"—and now he looked away from the huntsman and, gazing straight ahead, spoke in solemn, sorrowful tones—"there is one among us here tonight who . . . how shall I put it? how *can* I put it? . . . well, who would close the gates to you, Mr. Huntsman." And, like the brave, honest chap he was, he turned and looked the huntsman full in the face.

The huntsman returned the gaze steadily, but he felt his heart turn over, and despair seized him—he thought he had never heard such terrible, final words said to anyone. And now they had been said to him, to him. There wasn't a sound in the room.

"Yes?" said the huntsman at last. For clearly they were waiting for him to speak.

His host leaned forward and looked at someone far down the table. "All right, my Alpine friend," he said. "It is your turn now."

The huntsman saw the figure in the grey coat stand up. Ah! things were getting clearer. "My Alpine friend"—suddenly the huntsman understood: the grey fox could climb like a cat, something the red fox could never do. Often, when hunted, when pressed, the grey fox would take to a tree. . . . The red and the grey did not get along well together—the huntsman knew of a case where the red fox, being introduced for hunting purposes into a country where the grey predominated, was soon run out. And he recalled his host's remark a little while back: "He comes from another country—a country that we gave up. Sour grapes"—and how apt that was! And—now he saw the joke—"We never moved in his circles." And, despite the fear in his heart, the huntsman had to smile: for it was true that the red fox, as a rule, travelled fairly straight before hounds—witness this day!—while the grey was wont to circle, like some of the lesser breeds.

"—not exactly in training." The figure in the grey coat was speaking now, and it behooved the huntsman to listen to every word, for this one, for some unknown reason—unknown to the huntsman—was his mortal enemy.

"We had, of course, rather gorged ourselves," the little chap went on in a thin piping voice, "been up very late and all that sort of thing." The huntsman, hands clasped on the table in front of him, leaned forward, the better to hear. "We were prepared to sleep it off, as usual, when at an unconscionable hour, without drums or bugles, so to speak, the attack jumped off."

He paused, and the host took the opportunity to whisper in an aside to the huntsman, "He likes to put things in military jargon. You understand, of course."

"I understand," the huntsman said in a low voice. "I remember. Hounds were thrown in, about six in the morning."

"Exactly."

93

The figure in the grey coat suddenly burst out in much louder voice, "And I should like to seize this occasion to enter my strong protest against the modern so-called sneak attack. In former times no one would have considered beginning hostilities without a formal declaration of war, properly signed, sealed, and delivered. One marched against the enemy with banners flying, bands playing—fife and drum, anyway. ... Even on the very field of battle—you remember the classic example of Fontenoy—there was a certain ceremony, a show of *politesse*. I would inveigh——"

"He's off," someone said in not-too-hushed a voice, and at this point the host broke in:

"Yes, yes, my dear sir, we all know how he—er— the High Command"—he smiled at the concession he was making in adopting, for the moment, the other's language, "feels about beginning wars—not to mention war itself—without ultimatums, orders of mobilization, executive or legislative declarations, and other manifestations of an earlier and better civilization, so-called. Just as we knew the general consensus on the highest level with respect to the employment, *imprimus*, of unconventional—a rather mild term, be it said—weapons."

The figure in grey, arrested in full flight, by this ponderous stuff, bowed. "I felt very strongly in the matter," he explained.

"Naturally," said the host; "so did we all. But much is forgiven, as we know."

"Very well," the little chap in grey said. "I make no issue of the dawn, sneak attack, though in former times it was the custom to give the enemy a little time for the normal digestive processes——"

"Please proceed," the host said shortly.

The figure in grey stood in silence for a moment gazing down at the table. Then he looked up and began to speak quite simply and clearly and in a voice that seemed to come straight from his heart.

"I do not wish to bring the children into court, as the saying is. And if I say 'I, I, I,' as my story requires, it might seem that I were crying out in pain, 'Aie! Aie! Aie!' and that, as I see it, would be unfair to him whom all of you have found to be so scrupulously fair.

"So, with your permission, it shall be a story told in the third person, of . . . shall we call him Sergeant Gray? Indeed, I sometimes think of him as a lone trooper of the old Confederacy. . . ."

"You see," the host murmured for the huntsman's ear; "still the professional Southerner. We're all dam-yankees to him. They've forgiven, of course, by this time. But will they ever forget?"

"—recognized at once," the speaker was saying, "that he was, as usual, outnumbered: this time, some fifty to one. Outnumbered!" His voice rang out. "Who but we knew the dreadful import of that word? You hear the expression. 'The odds were against him.' Who but we knew what those odds could be? We alone——"

"Oh, come now!" a voice interrupted.

"What about the stag at eve?"

"Brer Rabbit," said another.

"Ferdinand."

"And poor sister Anise." This was apparently an old, outworn joke; no one laughed.

"Yes, yes," interrupted the host. To the speaker he said sternly. "That's all over the dam, sir."

"You'll have to pardon me, Mr. Chairman," the speaker said. "You see, Sergeant Gray was a very young recruit indeed and quite unaccustomed to the wrongs and snares of the world.

"Yes," he continued, "he'd rather gorged himself, as I've said, made rather a night of it like any other foolish, reckless young fellow, and so was in no condition to take the field of honour. A retrograde movement was definitely indicated.

"The order of battle, then——"

"We've had that," the host, or chairman as the speaker had called him, interrupted.

"Oh, yes. Well, the assault troops hit the cover at 0601. . . ."

"Dull as an Action Report," murmured the chairman.

" . the line of retreat," the speaker was saying, "ran in a wide arc from Ten-Acre Meadow——" when the chairman again interrupted:

"If you don't mind, sir, do spare us the details of the withdrawal. We all know the tune: 'Found at the Dingle Dell cover, ran to Locust Ridge, doubled back to Pine-Tree Ford. . . .' That's one form of torture we've usually been spared: the loser in our game is in no mood to go in for post-mortems. Perhaps we should count ourselves lucky. I am reliably informed that those who have to listen to this sort of thing consider it a fate worse than television."

The figure in grey bowed again—he might have been a rather flustered counsel dressed down by a biased judge.

"I understand, Mr. Chairman," he said humbly. "Only those who were there are really interested."

"Exactly."

The speaker was silent for a moment. Then he seemed to collect himself, as if for a great effort—as if indeed he were arguing a case and had not done very well and now must put everything he had into it.

"I wish I could say," he said in a stronger, clearer voice, "that Sergeant Gray ran rings round them, the way his daddy, the Colonel, used to do."

"Colonel!" said the chairman under his breath. "I'd like to see his commission!"

"But the sergeant was young and inexperienced," the speaker continued, "while the enemy was in great force and pressing hard. Well, gentlemen, I'm no General Francis Marion. . . ."

"His favourite campaigner," said the chairman aside to the huntsman; "naturally."

". . . nor do I pretend to compare the retrograde manœuvre to a Mons or Coruna or——"

The chairman gave a rude and audible chuckle.

"Oh, I know, I know," the speaker said with a mournful smile. "We flatter ourselves, we like to think we have done well, even when we have run away. But if I could tell you something of the terrain, of the overwhelming advantage held by the enemy in the matter of atmospheric conditions, comparative temperatures of earth and air, barometric pressure, percentage of precipitation——"

"You mean 'scent,' " a brutal voice interrupted. "Why so Nice Nelly?"

"—you would understand," the speaker went on, looking slightly reddish, "that at the end of an hour and twenty minutes——"

"One hour and forty-seven minutes," someone put in. "That's the figure on the plaque."

"Very flattering," the chairman said. "And just about as accurate as history ever is."

"One hour and twenty minutes," the figure in grey repeated firmly. "He claims no more than that. . . . Gentlemen, if I told you of these things—not forgetting the aid given the enemy by non-combatants, spectator sportsmen, filthy agriculturalists——"

" 'Dirt farmers' would be more polite," the chairman objected.

"I'm sorry," the speaker said quickly. "Anyway, many things seemed to conspire against Sergeant Gray that morning. The odds—the heavy odds we all have to face—were, so the sergeant thought, more weighted than ever. I like to think he put up a good show, though perhaps not a very long one. No, it did not take long for him to realize that he was utterly spent, in the last desperate stage of exhaustion. He had circled back to the Singing Brook"—the speaker broke off and threw a scared look towards the head of the table. "I'm sorry, Mr. Chairman; I mentioned the locale only because it's very close to the end——"

"Quite all right," the chairman said gruffly, in a kindlier voice.

"Sergeant Gray had his back to the wall," the speaker said earnestly, "and the swordsmen were coming at him from all sides——"

"I wish he'd stick to one era," the chairman murmured.

"—of course, the sergeant had his crampons along,"

the speaker said, slurring over the sentence in an apologetic tone. Defensively, he glanced round the table. "I realize that you gentlemen do not approve of certain articles of equipment that Sergeant Gray would naturally regard as indispensable——"

" '*Naturally*' is good," the chairman interrupted, smiling at the speaker. "It's not so much that we do not approve . . . isn't it, rather, a question of—shall we say, Government Issue?"

At this, a great laugh went up, but the speaker did not laugh or even smile. No, he was in Sergeant Gray's boots—with the climbing irons ready—his back against the wall, his breath gone, his little heart bursting, and the hosts of the enemy closing in.

"Ash or oak, he never knew," the speaker went on, and his voice shook a little, "and that was strange because the sergeant was a great one for knowing all the trees by name. But he never saw; up he went like a sailor up the shrouds in a sudden squall, and, scarcely a moment later, there was the enemy below.

"There were the hounds, at the foot of the tree. . . ."

Thus, abruptly, the speaker abandoned the fiction,

the thin disguise, the military jargon. The room was deathly still. Before—all during his speech—there had been whispers and low voices, the asides of the chairman, the sounds of matches being struck, of decanters sliding along the mahogany, but now there was not a sound, not a breath, and the silence was like a living thing in the room.

"There were the hounds, baying," he said again,

and the look in his eyes, the mounting pitch of his voice put you right there, in the ash or the oak, but not the bonny willow tree this time, with the tired grey fox gazing down on the death below. "Flinging and hurling themselves against the tree, they were," he went on, "and running up the tree a few steps, and falling back. And the cry, of course, all the time, the terrible cry. And the master and the huntsman and the two whippers-in, and all the field on their horses, all panting and laughing and congratulating the huntsman and marvelling at the wonderful, wonderful hounds—all, all, were there for, though the young fellow had done his best, he had not, as I have said, given them a very long run.

"This was the end—he knew enough for that, though this was his first brush with the enemy——"

He broke off. No one laughed at the terrible inadvertence; all knew that he had never intended a joke at such a time.

"Who could help knowing," he said quickly; "seeing what was there below? His heart was in his throat and the little wings were beating below his diaphragm, but he tried not to show a sign. He was swaying a little with the tree in the wind that had sprung up with the new day, and he felt a little tree-sick and also a little sorry for himself because he was so young and because he loved the wild free life he led, and—well, somehow it didn't seem altogether fair. The young *do* feel that way. And he wondered how the end would come. He had heard stories: once a tree had been cut down, once a lucky shot with a stone had found its mark. . . . And then, suddenly, he remembered that in all observed cases, the hounds, after marking the tree, had been taken some distance off . . . and what would happen then was that the sergeant, once somehow brought to the ground, would be given a few minutes' law, and the battle would be on again. And he wondered if he would have breath and heart enough for another go. And so, while clinging fast to the branch, he tried to relax and rest and restore his strength, the way a boxer does between rounds.

"But the minutes went on, and hounds were not taken away. And the fierce, yelping cry went on, although now some hounds stood silent, staring upwards, and some lay panting, and a few still kept charging the tree and climbing a few feet up and falling back again. Of the riders, almost everyone had dismounted, and three or four, having turned their horses over to others to be held, went about, looking— the sergeant soon realized—for missiles to throw at him. For now stones and heavy pieces of dead wood began to hurtle through the air. He clung tight to the tree's branch then, ready to duck and dodge, and all the while he looked quietly down at them. The two whippers-in were the most persistent—eager beavers always showing off, keeping up a continuous, wild bombardment—they were both poor shots—and the sergeant hated them the most, and the huntsman next.

"It seemed unfair, too," he said after a slight pause, "that they should be able to use the same ammunition over and over again. However, I don't think there was even a Marksman among them, for the sergeant never had to move. He just lay along the branch and, with both eyes wide, keeping constantly on the alert, watched them. And presently they tired of the game and left it and stood about in groups talking the situation over—the issue now, apparently, being in some doubt. And far up, near the top of the tree, the sergeant wondered what devilry they would be up to next.

"And then he saw that the huntsman had taken off his scarlet coat and yellow waistcoat and had come to the foot of the tree. Then the two whips were giving him a leg up to the lower branches. And now he began to climb—the huntsman himself! —and the sergeant looked down, very quiet and still, and, so far as he could see, the huntsman was unarmed—that is, he didn't have his hunting whip tied to him by the thong, or anything like that.

"The sergeant waited there, never moving, and his heart began to pound again and the fear came back on him. The man below him climbed steadily, pulling himself up from branch to branch; at the foot of the tree the hounds were milling once more, and their cry swelled to a new pitch of excitement. The little crowd of people stood like stones, silent now, staring up at the sergeant. Only the quiet horses seemed not to know or care what was going on.

"Through the bare branches, the sergeant could see, coming closer and closer, the dark blue velvet cap of the huntsman, the long, shirt-sleeved arms and gloved hands, pulling himself up and up. . . ."

The speaker stopped, and it seemed for a moment or two that the telling had become so unbearable to him that he could not go on. Someone near the head of the table cleared his throat, and the sound was like an explosion in the still room.

"And now"—the speaker seemed to be forcing the words out—"the huntsman came to the last branch, and his velvet cap was only a few feet below the branch where the sergeant lay—so close that the sergeant could hear the young man breathing—

panting a little from the hard climb. And the sergeant wondered what the next move would be . . . and then the huntsman looked up, and I swear he was smiling, and he said, "All right, old man," and he reached one arm up. . . .

"That's what he said to me," the speaker cried out, and his voice was a terrible thing to hear. "And

what did I think? Why, I thought he had come to save me! For he knew I would never jump down, and so he had come up. For some reason—I had no time to think about it all—he had changed, he was my friend, and so I jumped into his arms and put my head against his cheek, the way a dog does, in love, to his master, and he tore me from him and flung me to the hounds."

No one spoke or moved. The huntsman sat with bowed head, hands clasped in front of him. Then, at last, he heard his host, the chairman, say in a calm, detached voice:

"Well, Mr. Huntsman?"

The huntsman raised his head and looked straight at the figure in grey, who was still standing at his place.

"I had to blood my hounds," he said simply.

He would ask for nothing, say nothing more. That was the truth. How could he say here, among these, that it had been his first season as huntsman, that for the first three months they'd had no halfway good hunting, that hounds were getting lax, losing interest, skirting, babbling, rioting on rabbit or whatever jumped up in front of them? How could he say, here, that his livelihood, that life itself, depended upon his "showing sport" to the hunt members, to the field? And how could he tell the little chap in grey that the grey fox, in that country, was a nuisance rather than a huntable quarry? And say, outright, that this little chap hadn't really stood up to them, hadn't really put up a hunt, but had run round in a few panicky circles and then run up a tree? Gorged with food, so early in the morning— that was true. Well, that was the way wars were fought these days. Any one of these chaps in scarlet would have done better. . . .

These were the reasons for what he had done, and, though the huntsman remembered that morning so well—somehow it wouldn't go out of his mind— these reasons were sufficient for him. But he could not say so here, so he said again, qualifying the statement slightly out of deference to his host and the others there:

"I felt I had to blood my hounds."

Then, silence. Perhaps they were waiting for the figure in grey to reply, or for the chairman to say something, but neither said a word, and the silence went on and on.

And now the huntsman was sure that it was the end, for him—that the whole business, whatever it was, was over and finished, and he had lost out. He had been tried and found wanting, he had done a thing he never could undo, and there was no hope for him, ever any more. But how else, he asked himself bitterly, could he have fared in such a tribunal? If ever a court were rigged against a man! . . . There were those who thought it unfair that the victors should sit in judgment on the vanquished. What would they say to the other way round? Well . . . he turned and looked at his host—host, chairman, judge, all in one—and waited for the verdict.

Someone pushed back a chair, there was a slight disturbance—but the huntsman did not glance round. He heard, then, the tread of feet behind him, and a strange look—of joy? of triumph?—came into his host's face, and the next moment the huntsman felt an arm—thin and sinewy through the grey cloth—across his shoulders.

"It's all right, Mr. Huntsman," a voice said close

to his ear; "I understand. I should have remembered. You had your hounds to think of. Everything is all right." And the little chap in grey gave the huntsman a fierce squeeze—to hurt him with love—and went pattering back to his place at the table.

The chairman was getting to his feet. He held a brimming glass. Someone began to clap, and then the whole table burst into applause.

"To *Lieutenant* Gray!" the chairman cried. Cheers and more applause. Through the din the huntsman heard "—happy to announce . . . promotion . . . in the field, so to speak. . . ." The chairman leaned down and whispered to the huntsman, "Nothing could please him more."

Now all were getting up, calling for the decanters, filling glasses. The huntsman's neighbour on his right splashed some wine into the huntsman's glass. The huntsman rose, trying to hold his hand steady. All stood, facing the figure in grey, who was leaning back in his chair, his features fixed in a broad, foolish smile.

"Lieutenant Gray! Lieutenant Gray! Lieutenant. . . ." It was like a salute with all pieces not going off at once, quite unrehearsed.

"For he's a jolly good fellow," etc., etc.

Now they were all seated again except the chairman. The decanters were shoved round, glasses recharged. The chairman held out his empty one to the huntsman who filled it. The chairman raised his glass on high again, and the huntsman wondered what was coming—

"To the huntsman!"

All up on their feet again.

"The huntsman! The huntsman!" they all yelled. It was just as loud, just as enthusiastic. Oh, dear God! thought the huntsman, how shall I begin? For he was never any good, he hated to make a speech. The chairman leaned over to him.

"You may say 'Thank you,' " he said. "But no more. That is the rule."

"No speech?" the huntsman asked, and a great wave of relief went over him.

"No speech," the chairman said firmly, as he resumed his seat. "You might have guessed—if you had thought about it—that we would have no after-dinner speeches here."

Now all were seated again, and the huntsman rose. "Thank you," he said, looking all round the table till his eyes came to the little chap in grey. "Thank you," he said to him. That was all they expected. He sat down. He had never been so happy. . . .

But when talk was resumed and the decanters began to circulate again and they all looked like settling down for a night of it, the huntsman remembered how far he had to go and that he would have to get a car from kennels to come for him, and so he turned to his host and said:

"You've been awfully kind, and I can't tell you how much I've enjoyed this evening. But I shouldn't be sitting here, having such a good time, drinking your fine port." He smiled. "Why, pretty soon, I'll be looking for some close harmony——"

"We'll get around to that," his host assured him.

"Another evening, perhaps," the huntsman said, being most polite. "But now I'm afraid—if you'll excuse me—I'll have to see about getting home."

The chairman looked at him a long moment without speaking, and the huntsman could see now that the other was his friend, would always be—why, he could almost feel the kindness, yes, the love, the true loving kindness that was in the other's heart. And, for an instant, for a split second of time, the huntsman had the strange feeling that comes to almost all of us occasionally, which, for himself, he could never define or explain, that all this had happened before, long, long ago, in another world, another life: that his host and he had once sat thus together and that the other had spoken the very same words he spoke now:

"Home?" his host said in a low voice, for the huntsman's ear alone. "Surely when *he*"—with a nod he indicated the chap in grey down the other side of the table—"when he did what he did, said what he said, surely you realized, Mr. Huntsman. . . ." He looked at the huntsman hopefully. "We try to break it gradually," he murmured; "tonight is only the beginning . . . the tidings of great joy. . . ."

And then the huntsman knew.

IT WAS AN AFTERNOON such as the huntsman himself would have chosen: chill and grey, and growing colder as the winter sun declined—a good hunting day; good for scent. The Wednesday fixture had been postponed till the next day, and some of the more fanatical sportsmen resented it a little, for a real freeze was on the way and if they'd been able to go out this day, they'd have probably had a real buster—and after such rotten luck all season. The ground, the clay roads, were hard, but not frozen and you could have really flown over the grass and made good time in the bottom lands. The trees still looked like metal—stark and, for the most part, bare of even dead leaves. No reason, yet, to look for the stinking violets, which another huntsman so dreaded to see because they meant the season of hunting would soon be over. There were some violets to be seen that afternoon, but they were the hothouse kind, like the other flowers, now heaped near the open grave.

When the short service in the cemetery was over and the people began, slowly, with muted voices to walk away, a rather tall, slim girl, dressed in black, still stood there, a little way off, beyond the bank of flowers, gazing in an unseeing way at the grey-cloth-covered coffin, which rested on slings at the surface of the ground and which would not be lowered to its resting place till all had gone.

Standing there, alone, not leaving with all the others, she might have made herself conspicuous, without ever meaning to, so an elderly gentleman, dressed in the height of sombre fashion, went over to her and took her arm and guided her down to the pebbled path that led out through the open gates.

As they went in silence along the path, a much younger man dropped back and joined them, and the older man, seeing that the girl and the newcomer did not know one another, made the introduction. He said, then:

"It was good of you to come all the way here."

"It was the least I could do," the young man said shortly, brushing it aside. "What a terrible piece of luck! The old horse, too."

"Yes."

"Were you out?—I've heard so many different versions. . . ."

"Naturally," said the older man. "You know how such things get distorted. Yes, I was out, but not at"—he hesitated and then said—"not when it happened. The young lady was there—she and one of the whips stopped hounds and brought them home —it was almost dark, you know."

"Oh, yes." The young man looked at the girl.

"It was a gate," she said in a low, singularly lovely voice. She paused.

The young man thought that for some reason it was terribly hard for her, so he said:

"Never mind, if it's too—if it's too——"

"Oh, no," she said quickly. "You were his friend —I heard him speak of you once—and you should know what really happened. It was a gate," she said again. "At each end, at each post, there was a stick——"

"That's what I heard," the young man broke in: "that extensions were nailed to each post and a strand of wire ran across from one to the other. Electrified, I suppose, and fixed that way so as not to break the connection——"

"No," the older man said, "it was not electric wire. That's the queer thing."

"It was barbed wire," the girl said; "I saw it—unbroken."

"It was you, who—who——"

"After we got the hounds in the van," she said, "and he did not come, I went back to the gate——"

"Alone?" the young man said almost involuntarily.

"I thought the whip should go back with hounds," she said simply. "I got help, quite soon. . . ."

"But—but"—he turned to the older man—"what was it? A trap? What was the idea? Was the country closed?—someone sore at the hunt——?"

"Not that we know of," the other said. "It wasn't our regular country, of course, though we had it registered. We haven't yet found out the reason for the wire being that way—the owner of the land's off in the wilds somewhere and no one knows yet who put up the wire."

"*I'd* like to find him," the young man said.

"I have a theory," the older man went on, "that no harm was meant; on the contrary. My theory is that whoever was putting up the wire that day didn't have wire-cutters with him, so he just carried this wire over the gate, but put it high enough so that a car or a man in a wagon, say, or on a horse, could pass underneath, through the open gate——"

"It sounds crazy," the younger man said. "He could have cut the wire somehow. Or carried it underground——"

"Have you ever tried to cut heavy wire without wire-cutters—or at least an axe or a hack saw, or something besides a hammer? As for burying it—apparently it had been put up very recently, and you could hardly scratch the ground this last month. I can't think of any other explanation—it was a temporary, makeshift job and would have been changed. And you could see the wire plain enough—in the daylight. It was a trap, all right—but only in the dark, in the dusk."

"I've heard of some queer ones," the younger man said, and left it at that. But being one of those whose chief interest in life is fox hunting, he could not forbear to ask the question: What were they going to do about the rest of the season?

"We're going on hunting, of course," the older man replied. "It's what he would have wanted—can you imagine him ever missing a day? Our first whip

—came since you've hunted here—is taking over temporarily. It won't be the same—it'll never be the same, but we'll have to make do, for this year. We're meeting tomorrow, by the way. I'd be glad to mount you. I have a young chestnut I've just bought, rather green, but——"

"That makes me sure I have to get home," the young man said to the girl, smiling at her, trying to inject a little note of lightness into the sad business. To the older man, he said, "I saw . . ." and he named two or three names of people they both knew well who had also come from afar.

"Oh, yes," the other said. "They came from all over the place. And from . . . well, from many walks of life besides the hunting field and the hunt race meeting and so on. It was quite a tribute."

"I never knew a man who had more friends," the young man said. Happening to glance at the girl, he saw, to his dismay, the tears welling up in her eyes. The older man, unseen by her, gave the other a meaning look, raised his eyebrows, and shook his head slightly; all, apparently, to tell him not to go on with that. So the young man said nothing more,

and they walked in silence to the gates, and there the young man said good-bye to them and went on his way.

"Have you a car here?" the older man asked the girl. "Can I run you home? My car's just around the corner."

"Home?" the girl said. "Do I have to go home?" She said no more than that, but it was her way, he knew, of telling him that her father and she did not get along. On this day, in this unguarded moment, she would tell him, who was her friend, but she would tell no one else.

"There are several houses you can go to," he said, "where drinks will be served during the afternoon and far into the night. I am due now at the——"

"I couldn't."

"You mustn't blame them," he said, watching the people getting into cars and the cars moving slowly along the narrow road, just as after a race meeting, a steeplechase, a game. "It seems to make things easier," he went on, "though I've found it's rather worse, in the end."

"If he hadn't sent me away!" she said suddenly

in a low voice, staring at him. "If I had been there, perhaps I could have——"

"Done nothing," the older man said firmly. "It was, as we know, instant.

"Of course he sent you away," he went on, almost angrily. "He didn't want you riding at a four-and-a-half-foot gate, built like a blockhouse, at the end of *that* day, on *that*—you'll have to excuse me—on *that* crazy animal. Will you tell me, please, how you ever got through that run?"

And then, since she did not answer—and what could she have said?—but stood there, gazing forlornly down at the wintry earth, he spoke out in real anger.

"Look here! I'm going to tell you something no one's ever dared say to you: Some girls can ride crazy, fool horses and get away with it—sometimes. They're the kind that were brought up in a stable— probably slept in a loose-box. But you—*you* probably never saw a horse till a few years ago—I understand they're extinct where you come from." At this she did laugh, the way he loved to hear her laugh—she was kind to even his poorest jokes. "How long have you ridden?" he asked in an angry voice again. "Two years. How long have you hunted? One season, before this one. Oh, I know. I've looked into it thoroughly. Why? Because the very first day, I thought, 'There's a girl I'd like to have for a daughter' (if I'd ever married), and, God forgive me! I admired (and I hated, for your sake) the way you persisted, riding straight, never going round, never avoiding a fence, though half-scared to death—oh, I know all about it!—most of the time."

She looked up at him, and he could see that she had been crying before—before today, this afternoon—and the crying had rather marred her beauty —he always thought of her as beautiful—for the moment. But time, he knew (being an old man and having gone through many of these things), would cure all, and after a while it would mean no more to her than something to remember with a proper sadness.

"It's something I've got to do," she said. He collected his thoughts. She meant that in spite of what he had said to her, and what she must know in her heart, she would go on—go on with something that to him was one of the delights of the world, to her a dread and awful duty.

"Very well," he said, beaten. "If you feel that way. . . . But get rid of that dangerous beast. There are plenty of good safe conveyances——"

"No," she interrupted, shaking her head. "That's part of it. I'm hunting him tomorrow."

He could hardly believe his ears. Then he was so angry that he burst out, "Well, it will be your own——" and stopped just in time, for it was the last expression to use on such an occasion.

"Will you run me home?" she said, looking at him, and her eyes were despairing, and he saw—what he had not seen clearly before—that here was a human soul absolutely lost in grief. He had heard the cruel gossip, how the master's daughter was hopelessly gone on the huntsman, and suddenly it struck him that this thing had hit her harder, oh, much harder, than he had supposed. It could be that from a hopeless, worshipping kind of love, which now could never know any fulfilment, one might never completely recover. Could be.

So, he would take her home—where she did not want to go. He tried to look ahead, into the future. With all his heart he hoped that something good would happen for her.